Spring Story

Written and Illustrated by Dee Smith

Copyright © 2015

<u>**Visit Deesignery.com**</u>

CW01086312

Spring is lovely and it comes every year.

Spring's arrival is sure to bring with it, Spring cheer.

A rabbit does a few high hops.

From a bud, a flower pops.

The Sun gives a delightful shine.

Small animals gather before they start to dine.

A bird sings a lovely song.

Other animals join and sing along.

Soft white snow begins to melt.

Now crisp green grass can be seen and felt.

On some spring days, a few raindrops
create a mist.

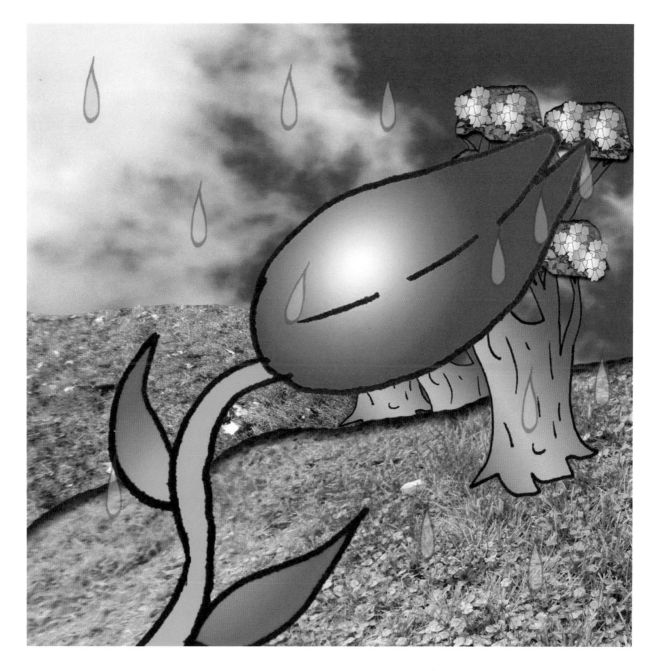

They give the ground a cool wet kiss.

Petals soar in the warm air.

Small bees and flowers form a pair.

The whole scene is beautiful, every little thing.

Ah, the joys we get from Spring!

Bonus Book

As a special thanks to you for selecting this book!

Everyone gather around the Spring Pond!

Of the cool waters, the animals are fond!

A rabbit hops in and it creates a splash.

When the animals play, the water does dash.

A small bird puffs his feathers out.

A bullfrog gives a croak and pout.

A fly lands gracefully on a lily pad.

A bird stops to greet both his Mom and Dad.

A fish in the pond takes a graceful dive.

A bee soars overhead to a nearby hive.

A beaver collects branches to construct a home.

It looks like a large wooden leaf covered dome.

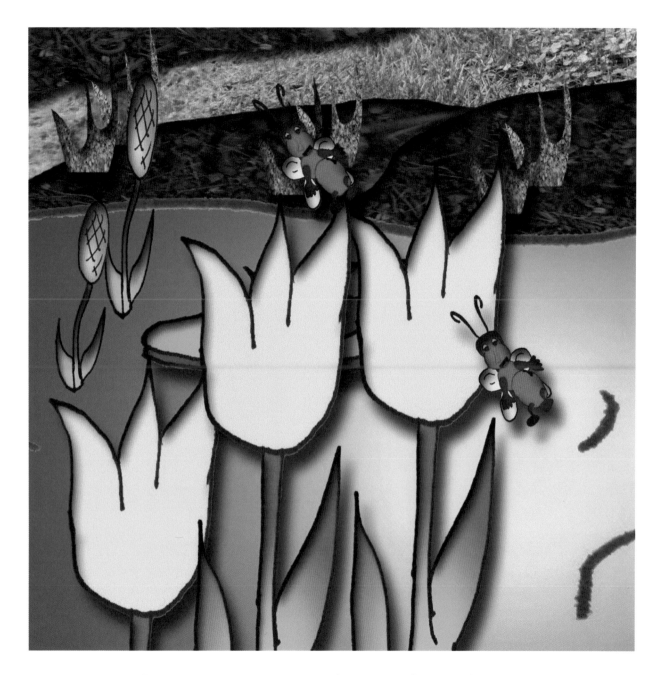

Around the pond's edges a few flowers have sprouted and grown.

A sweet sugary scent is left in the air after a soft wind has blown.

All of the animals are delighted that spring is here.

It is a season that we all hold dear!

Thank You!

Thank you so much for reading this book.
It means the world to me!
If you liked the book I would much appreciate if you would write a Review on Amazon. I am so thankful for each and every person supporting my dream of being a writer for children. Because you have read this book, yes that means YOU too! Thanks Again!
Stay tuned for more titles on my website Deesignery.com

Regards,
Dee

About the Author:

My name is Dee Smith. I am an Author and Illustrator. My hobbies include graphic design, puppetry, balloon twisting, drawing and of course writing. I am dedicated to my mission of keeping children entertained in fun and innovative ways.

See what the Buzz is all about!
Take a journey to Bee-ville

Read this fun series about a small bee that goes on big adventures and learns along the way!

Printed in Great Britain
by Amazon